ALL ALONG

RICK W. FRENCH

Order this book online at www.trafford.com
or email orders@trafford.com

Most Trafford titles are also available at major online book retailers.

The Show Choir names of "Panache"
and "Young Originals" are used by
courtesy of the South Montgomery School Corporation.
Southmont High School
Crawfordsville, Indiana
"Rock On" Mounties!
Printed in Victoria, BC, Canada.

ISBN: 978-1-4269-2870-3 (sc)

*Our mission is to efficiently provide the world's finest, most comprehensive
book publishing service, enabling every author to experience success.
To find out how to publish your book, your way, and have it available
worldwide, visit us online at www.trafford.com*

Trafford rev. 3/26/10

 www.trafford.com

North America & international
toll-free: 1 888 232 4444 (USA & Canada)
phone: 250 383 6864 ♦ fax: 812 355 4082

DEDICATION

*I would like to thank my family for always
standing beside me on the journey of life.
They have always been beside me at every curve.*

In Memory:

In memory of Robert W. French.
You left us way too soon.

CHAPTER 1

July 21, 1982 was not your typical summer day for Collin and Ali Tucker. They were driving to the hospital to bring their first child into the world. This pregnancy had been a difficult one for Ali. She had been bedridden for the past 4 weeks. They had been trying for a child the past 3 years. They were just about to go to an adoption agency to begin their family when they learned of their pregnancy.

It had been a difficult time for the Tuckers. Collin had recently lost his job with the phone company, a victim to corporate downsizing. An old high school teammate of

Collins had gone into factory work directly out of high school. When he heard about Collin, he called and said he could get him a job at the factory if he so desired. With Ali being pregnant, Collin took the job, even though he had made a promise to himself that he would never go the route his father had gone.

Several employees at the factory recognized Collin on his first day. Collin had been a very popular local high school athlete that seemed to have the world by the tail. Everything he attempted, he excelled in. He had been scouted and offered scholarships to several universities, but had turned them down to marry his high school sweetheart, Ali.

The evening of July 21 at 11:20, Ali gave birth to Cody, a very healthy 8 lbs 8 oz. spitting image of Collin. They had not known of the child's gender prior to delivery. Of course they both said as long as the child was healthy it really didn't matter. But both were secretly pulling for their own gender as most first time parents do.

Ali's desire was to be a stay at home mom, just as her mother was. Collin, though not happy with factory work, excelled as always and worked his way into a supervisor's position during his first year. Cody was walking now and getting into everything in their small two bedroom home. Ali was hinting to Collin about wanting another child, but their house was just too small. They decided to look for a bigger house in the "city" where the factory was located. Most people would not have given this move of 15 miles much thought. But for the Tuckers, moving from their small hometown of 400 people, moving to the county seat, a town of 15,000 people, was a big move.

The three bedroom ranch home was like a mansion to both of them. Neither had been raised in anything this nice. Ali couldn't believe her house actually had two separate bathrooms! Even though Collin liked the house, he could see his future and knew he was now "stuck" in a place where he swore he would never tread.

As Cody continued to grow, Collin could easily detect the athletic abilities he possessed. Like all fathers, Collin was looking well into the future for Cody and could see great things ahead. Collin's father had been a good athlete, and Collin had surpassed him. Now Collin was hoping for the same with Cody, making it to the next level.

CHAPTER 2

Three years had passed when Ali discovered she was pregnant with their second child. Cody, now being 4, didn't quite understand at first. This time, Ali wanted to learn the gender. And this time around, her secret prayer of a girl had been answered. Cali came into the world on October 26, at a healthy 8 lbs.

On the day that Ali and Cali came home from the hospital the look on Cody's face was that of pride and protection. Cody was making sure that she was never alone, and when she cried out, he became visibly upset.

Collin was making comments already about Cody being the big brother protecting his little sis.

That following spring a new family was moving in three houses down. The Tuckers were watching as the moving van pulled in and started unloading. Ali noticed a small bicycle and a child's bedroom suit being unloaded. The following day Ali walked down to introduce herself. When she knocked on the front door, a young boy, about the same age as Cody, came running. Directly behind him was the mother. She opened the door with a smile and stuck out her hand towards Ali.

She introduced herself, "Hello, I am Audrey and this is my son Alan." Ali took a hold of her hand and shook it, "Hi, I am Ali Tucker and I live three houses down.

I just wanted to welcome you to the neighborhood." She looked down to the young boy, "How old is your son?" "Well, Alan is 4 but going on 14!" Audrey giggled as she spoke. "That's great, we have a 4 year old boy as well, but he is only going on 5", Ali said with a big grin.

We should get them together. Cody could use another boy to play with. We also have a 6 month old girl, Cali.

"That sounds great. Alan is our one and only and he could use a playmate as well."

A few days had passed and the spring weather was beginning to break. Cody was outside riding his bicycle in the backyard when his mother came out to hang clothes on the line. As Ali was turning around to grab some more clothes from the basket, she noticed Alan riding his bike towards them. There was a section behind the tract house that everyone referred to as the "alley."

As Alan turned into the yard, Ali looked towards his house and noticed Audrey outside watching him. They both waved at each other as Alan hoped off his bike.

Alan was wearing glasses, and his body was not nearly as developed as Cody's for a 4 year old. Ali listened as they started talking to each other. Ali could easily tell from the beginning that the only thing Cody had in common with Alan was age.

CHAPTER 3

Later that summer, Audrey walked down the alley with Alan to visit. Ali was outside working in the garden when they approached. She walked over to the door and yelled inside for Cody, saying Alan was there. He was inside watching a baseball game on TV. While the boys played outside, Ali invited Audrey inside for some iced tea. "This is the best iced tea I have ever tasted Ali! I wish mine tasted this good."

"It's not a big secret really. I just sun brew it, that's about it honestly."

Audrey took another sip, sitting the glass down. "Ali, I wanted to invite you to go to church with us this Sunday. We found a great church, with a lot of younger children. It's just a great bunch of people. I have even joined the choir, and I can't carry a tune in a bucket!" Ali had been raised in a church life, but had not gone since they had moved to town. Raising two children seemed to take over all their time. Collin worked a lot of overtime on weekends as well, trying to make ends meet with two children on one income. "Thank you for asking. We have wanted to get back into going, but we haven't even looked yet." The following Sunday, the Tucker's accompanied the Montgomery's to Mount Union Christian Church. They seemed to fit right in, and soon thereafter joined the church. Ali even joined Audrey in the choir. It didn't take long before everyone realized that Ali had a true gift of singing, and she soon had the number one seat.

CHAPTER 4

Over the next few years the families didn't have a lot in common other than church on Sundays and the occasional backyard summer visits. Cody was turning 9 years old this summer. This was an important age for him as now he could play little league baseball. Collin had signed up to coach to ensure Cody would have the best chance to excel. He thought it might be a good gesture to ask Alan if he wanted to play. He said he could be on Cody's team, and he could always ride with them to games and practices. Even though Alan appeared to have more in common with sister Cali, Cody asked him. Alan had always been a bookworm and would rather read than play. Surprisingly to Cody, Alan said yes.

During the first practice the majority of the boys had some talent at hitting and catching the ball. Alan, on the other hand, didn't even know the positions on the field. The boys were being boys and starting making fun of Alan. All he could do was hang his head in embarrassment.

On the way home Collin told Alan that he would be just fine, anyone could learn to play the game. Collin knew that Alan's father, Clyde, didn't have an athletic background. He always pushed Alan towards scholastics. The next few practices didn't seem to change much. Alan had learned the positions, but just didn't seem to have any athletic ability in his bones.

During the first game of the season, Collin was coaching third base while his team was at bat. The leadoff hitter, Cody, stepped in to bat for the first time of his little league career. The first pitch was high, way out of the strike zone and Cody swung, missing the ball by several feet. Collin kicked at the dirt in disgust, and then yelled at Cody to keep his eye on the ball. Cody looked to the dirt in the batter's box. The next two pitches were not even close to the plate, and Cody swung at both striking out on three pitches. Collin screamed and yelled as Cody hung his head and walked back to the dugout. The entire team was sitting in silence as Cody walked in. Alan never got to play that game, sitting and listening as Collin continued calling out Cody in front of everyone as his team went down in defeat.

The next day Alan rode his bike down the alley to Cody's house. Cody still had that defeated look from the game the previous day. Alan tried talking to him. "My dad told me last night that sometimes when parents become upset, they say things they don't really mean. Look at the bright side Cody, your dad was at least there! Mine was at work!" Alan was making a young man's attempt to reach out the only way he knew how. Cody just blew him off and went back inside the house.

The rest of the baseball season continued down the same beaten path. Cody did get better with each game. Even though he turned out to be on the best players in the entire league, his dad/coach continued riding him all season long. Alan did get to play towards the end of the season, with only his mother in the stands.

CHAPTER 5

The elementary school years were dwindling down. They had reached grade five. Cody was now playing a lot of sports and playing them all very well. All of the other kids looked up to him. He was also the "big brother" of the cute new girl, first grader Cali.

During grade five, all the students had to learn to play an instrument. Alan, who had already been taking violin lessons for 2 years now, was suddenly the most popular kid. Not only could he play the violin, he played it very well. For the first time in Cody's life, the other kids weren't looking at him. Cody went home and told his parents that day he wanted to take guitar lessons. Cody's father, Collin, didn't like the idea and said he needed to focus more on sports. Ali, on the other hand, thought Cody should learn how to play and said she would ask around. She found a man in the church choir that agreed to give him lessons for free. Over the next several months, Cody never missed a practice. He had his mind made up that he would never be "one upped" again. The instructor was amazed at just how well he took to the guitar. The guitar seemed to be a natural fit in his arms.

Cody kept his secret from everyone about taking guitar lessons. He even had to deny his little sisters "rumors" of him learning how to play.

The fifth grade basketball team was doing very well with Cody playing. None of the other kids could keep him from scoring. Grade five was even beating grade six in practice. Cody was again on top of the world, being the center of attention.

During a teacher/parents conference, Ali and Collin were speaking with Cody's teacher. During this conversation, they were advised that Cody seemed to be slipping with his grades overall. They were advised that his attention to detail had dropped greatly. He was struggling in several areas and that she was in fact concerned. If he didn't show some improvement, summer school would not be out of the question. His dad tried speaking with Cody, but it became a yelling session instead. Ali tried talking with him the next day and Cody just shut down.

Cody was pretending at school that everything was just fine. Only his parents and teacher knew about his grades. With summer school hanging directly over his head, he knew he had to do something. For the first time in his life, he asked Alan for help. Alan was more than up for the challenge. He wanted his friendship to continue with Cody as he was one of the most popular kids in school. Cody told him that nobody could know about it, and they would have to meet secretly. Alan agreed without question. During their "private" meetings, Alan would use sports to relate to the subjects they were studying. This approached kicked into high gear and seemed to work out well. After their study sessions, they would play the violin and guitar and have their own "jam sessions" laughing and sharing in the moment.

The secret friendship grew, but Cody didn't want anyone else to know about it. Even though he didn't completely understand why, Alan agreed.

CHAPTER 6

Their arrangement continued all through junior high. At school, Cody would treat Alan as a complete stranger. Alan was "a geek with no future" according to the "in crowd." The only time Cody would be seen with Alan, was behind closed doors.

The eighth grade was upon them, just one year away from being in high school.

During warm-ups for a basketball game, Cody could not find his parents in the stands. His parents always sat in the same seats in the gym. The game was about to start when the coach called Cody back to the locker room. Cody knew something wasn't right as it was just the coach and the principle present. His coach started out by taking a deep breath, swallowed hard, then looked at him. "Cody, your parents have been involved in a car accident. We need to get you to the hospital right away." Cody looked to the floor and tears fell off his cheek. Cody quickly changed out of his basketball uniform and walked out of the locker room. He was met by Alan along with his mother Audrey. She had heard about the accident and grabbed Alan and drove to the school as fast as they could. She took Cody to the hospital. She told Cody that Cali was at her friend's house, and that she was being taken care of.

When they arrived at the hospital Audrey asked for the doctor and informed him that Cody was in the waiting room. The doctor told Audrey that his mother, Ali, was banged up and cut, but she was going to be fine. His father, Collin, however was hurt worse with broken bones and will be needing surgery.

They went to the waiting room to speak with Cody. He just sat there, without emotion as if in shock. The doctor told him that his mother would be released the next day. Audrey advised him she would make sure the kids were taken care of. Cody would spend the night with them, while Cali spent the night at her friends not aware of what had happened.

During the night Alan could hear Cody crying in the bed next to him. Alan again reached out to Cody in a time of need. At first Cody just tuned Alan out. But as time went on into the night, Alan did indeed calm Cody down enough to where he would eventually fall asleep.

The following day Ali was released from the hospital. She had several stitches and was confined to a wheelchair. Cody guarded her as if he were in the secret service.

She was going to have a full recovery; however it was just going to take her some time. Cody was suddenly the "man of the house" since his dad was still in the hospital.

Cody stepped up taking care of everything around the house. He was like a father for Cali as well. Here he was, a 14 year old boy, taking care of two woman and worried he was about to lose his best friend in the world, his dad Collin.

CHAPTER 7

The church had members stopping by each day. Most of them brought food and some brought flowers. Collin was still in the hospital. His body wasn't recovering as quickly as expected. Ali was now out of the wheelchair, but her movement about the house was still restricted. Over the course of the next several weeks Cody and Cali took care of the household chores. Collin was about to be released from the hospital, but faced a long road for complete recovery.

The day Collin came home, he asked Cody how his baseball season was going. With everything he had facing him, he was thinking about Cody and baseball. For the first time Cody was playing for a coach other than his dad. He was enjoying a coach that was quick to comment on the good things, and not call out the bad things as much as his dad had done. Cody was responding well to this new environment. Ali wasn't sure if it was from the new coach, or the fact that Cody was trying so much harder to prove to dad he could play. Cody was quick to report all the game details back to dad as soon as he got home from the game. Collin was still finding the road to recovery to be very, very bumpy.

During the summer evenings, Alan would come over to Cody's house and they would go down into the basement and play their instruments. Both of them were getting very comfortable and sounded very good together. Cody even had Cali joining them at times, singing songs that he had written. Cali was taking after her mother and she could sing any type of music and sing them well. Even though Cody enjoyed these sessions, he demanded that they didn't tell anyone about them. He always had his image on the front page.

CHAPTER 8

Cody had turned 15 during the summer. His body was changing almost daily it seemed. He had grown 4 inches during the summer and was now standing at a lean 6' 1". Collin had hoped that Cody would surpass his 6' 4" frame, and now it appeared that just might be the case. Not only his body had changed, but his voice did as well. Gone were the crackles and high pitched tones that he had at times. His deep voice almost seemed to have been placed in his vocal cords overnight.

Even though Alan was the same age, his growth spurt was still yet to hit, if it ever would.

Alan was still fitting the description of "geek" to the fullest. He still wore the old style horned rimmed glasses with his shirts still buttoned all the way to the top.

The first day of high school was as different for Cody and Alan as night and day.

The upper classman had been waiting on Cody to arrive to help with their teams. The coaches had been talking about him for a couple of years now. They wanted him just as badly.

Of course all the girls knew of Cody as well. It was almost like a rock star and stopped by the school to visit. As for Alan, he was just one of the many. He was pushed aside by the upper classman and only the "geeks" would speak to him. Nobody knew, and nobody really cared, that Alan had one of the highest IQ's of any incoming freshman in the school's history. The treatment he received was just the same ol' routine for him. Alan knew his place and kept to himself. His only time of self reflecting was when he would pass Cody in the hallway, and Cody would act as though he didn't even know him.

It didn't take Cody long before he was "hooked up" with a junior cheerleader. Even though they seem to be a good match, everybody knew that Cody was using her since she had her driver's license and a car. No more parent drop off's to school for Cody, he was being escorted by a cheerleader.

Football practice was in full swing now. The talk of the school was about how good Cody was. He was already named as the starting quarterback. Cody's ego was growing at the same rate his body had during the summer.

The first game of the season was against a conference rival, Mt. Comfort. Mt. Comfort had won the conference the year before and had even gone to the state finals where they were beaten at the last second. They only lost three players from the year before and they were expected to be back at the state finals again. The local newspaper had an article about the game every night for a week prior to the game. The only person I think was more excited about the game than Cody was his father Collin. Collin still hadn't recovered from the accident. All though he was back at home, he was still confined to a wheelchair. His body just wasn't healing.

Collin was rolled out next to the fence in the end zone so he could see the entire field. When the game started, he waved to Cody. Cody covered his heart with his hand, and waved back.

The game was played out as if it had been written down like one of Cody's songs.

Everything fell into place. They upset Mt. Comfort, with Cody setting school and state records in his very first high school game.

CHAPTER 9

The next four games were blue prints of the season opener. They were undefeated and Cody was blowing up every record in sight.

Just before game six, Collin had severe pains in his lower stomach. Cody had just left the house with his girlfriend when Collin bent over in his wheelchair. Ali had to call for an ambulance to get him to the hospital. She didn't want Cody to know anything before the game. During warm-ups, Cody noticed that his dad was not in the end zone like always. He went through the motions of the pregame drills, but his mind and eyes kept drifting to the empty end zone.

Cody looked for his sister Cali in the stands, but couldn't find her either. He ran over to his girlfriend and asked where everybody was at. She just shrugged her shoulders saying she had no idea.

The game was ready to start and Cody knew he had to focus on getting ready to play. They did in fact win the game, but it was not one Cody's best performances.

As soon as the game was over, he went to the stands again looking for his sister and parents. Then he noticed Alan walking towards him at a fast pace. Cody could see the trouble in Alan's eyes and grabbed him by the shoulders. Alan just told him to quickly change, and he and his mother would drive Cody to the hospital. Cody's mind quickly raced back to the last time this scene played out and both of his parents were hurt in the car accident. Alan told him that his dad got sick and his mother and sister had taken him to the emergency room.

As soon as he walked into the emergency room, his sister Cali came running towards him. His mother Ali was right behind her. Ali informed Cody that his dad had suffered severe pains in his stomach and had to be brought in. He asked where he was, and Ali pointed to a pulled curtain. Cody started towards the curtain when he was stopped by a nurse. After learning who he was, he was let in.

Collin was lying on a bed with oxygen tubes attached to his nose. He seemed to be struggling for breath as he spoke. His first words – "Well did you win?" Cody just shook his head yes and asked how he was feeling. Collin shook his head no, whispering "not well- it hurts when I breathe."

Collin was admitted and had to stay a few days for tests. Cody tried to get back to "normal" at school, but his heart and mind were back at the hospital.

Collin was going back and forth to the hospital every three days for more tests.

He was taking several different prescriptions for the pain. He would fade in and out and not make a lot of sense at times when he spoke. He had just taken several pills before Cody got home from school on a Friday night. They were having their last home game that night. Cody, even though he knew better, was still hoping that his dad could make it to the game. As he walked into the room,

Collin was under the influence of the narcotics and just went crazy on Cody. He wasn't making any sense about anything. He told Cody he wasn't as good as he once was. He said that he would never amount to anything. Cody, with tears in his eyes, just turned and walked out of the room.

The game that night was just a blur to Cody. They did win the game, but again he didn't have a good performance.

The following week was absolute madness around the school. The football team was undefeated with one game left to play. The newspaper and other media were casting this team as one of the best ever. In each article written, Cody's name was brought up as the reason for the success.

During Wednesday night's practice, as Cody was running drills, his mother pulled into the parking lot. Cody noticed the car, and at first thought Cali had something going on at school. Then he saw his mom and Cali get out, and walk towards the football field. Cody felt pain in his stomach like a linebacker had just kicked him.

He threw the ball down and walked towards them. He first noticed Cali as she was crying. He looked at his mother and seen that she had been as well. "WHAT? WHAT?" Cody yelled at them. His mother just said that the doctor had just told her that Collin had cancer, and he didn't have long to live. Cody fell to his knees. He covered his head with his hands and was weeping as the coach walked over. Ali told him of the news. He knelt down beside Cody placing his arm over his shoulder pads. His coach tried consoling Cody, but it didn't help much. Ali just said, "Come on Cody, we need to get to the hospital."

CHAPTER 10

On the drive to the hospital Cody never spoke a word. His mind was racing over the past 15 years. He was trying his best to hold back the tears. He knew he was a strong kid, but he wasn't ready for something like this.

When they arrived at the hospital, an intern was at the desk. Cody approached the desk and the intern turned around slowly reading a chart. He looked over the clip board to Cody, "hey aren't you Cody Tucker?" Cody shook his head yes, but his eyes were saying other things. The intern then realized the patient in the other room had the same last name. "Oh, mmmm, sorry Cody. I didn't realize Collin was your dad." The intern walked him over to the room, then left to get Collin's chart.

Cody walked in slowly holding his breath. Collin was sitting up in bed, watching TV. Cody walked around the bed and sat down beside him. His dad asked where his mother was at. Cody said that she was with Cali in the waiting room. After a few moments of silence, Cody asked his dad, "so what are they telling you?" Collin sipped on his soda, and then looked at him."Well, they said my body wasn't healing from the accident like it should have because I have bone cancer. They tell me if I hadn't had the accident, they never would have found it."

Collin continued, "but that's the only good news." Cody looked into his eyes and couldn't speak. "They are telling me I don't have long, not long at all to live." Cody took a deep breath, "like how long is not long?" Collin was doing his best at trying to keep it together in front of Cody. "MMM, well they say I could go anytime I guess!" Cody burst out into tears and weeping hard. Collin reached out his hand and grabbed Cody's. "Listen to me son. It could be worse!" Cody glared at him, "What do you mean it could be worse? They just told you that are dying. How could anything be worse?" Collin squeezed Cody's hand, "son, it could be you lying here instead of me. Now that would be worse." Cody dropped his head, crying harder than ever before.

It was amazing to Cody on how cavalier his dad was about his own demise. Collin continued talking with him. Telling him to be a good kid, stay out of trouble, get his degree and see where sports would take him. Cody listened to every word. He told him that he would do his best to make something of himself. He also promised to take care of his mother and sister Cali. They talked well into the night. His mother and Cali gave him the time he needed with his dad. The next day, Thursday, Cody and Cali both went to the hospital instead of school. They both spent the entire day with their dad in his room. They talked about old times, how things are messed up today, and what they should do to fix the problems. That afternoon, there was a knock on the door and it was Alan. He came walking into the room carrying a scrapbook. He handed it to Collin. "I thought you might want to see this sir. When we started high school, I thought it would be neat to keep a scrapbook. I know you messed a few games, all the news articles and box scores are in it." Cody didn't have any idea that Alan was doing that. Cali jumped up and gave him a hug.

Just before leaving, Alan handed Cody another envelope. Cody just looked at it.

"What's this?" Alan said it was his homework assignments from the last two days. "Don't worry, it's all done and you are welcome for the A."

Friday morning, just before school, Ali got a call from the hospital. They wanted the family there as soon as possible. When they arrived in the room, a nurse and two doctors were standing over Collin. They turned to Ali and said we are sorry, but the end is real near. It will be any minute now. Cody pushed them aside and stood beside the bed grabbing his father's hand. Collin's eyes were open, but were glazed over. When Cody spoke, he could feel his father's hand tighten. His mother and sister went to the other side of the bed. Everyone was crying, and Collin struggled for breath. Within a couple of minutes, Collin took at deep breath, and let it out slowly, and the monitors went flat lined. Cody reached up and then closed his dad's eyes for the last time. Collin was only 52 years old.

Cody knew his dad would want him to play in the game that night. He was undecided if to make an attempt or not. He knew his team needed him, but his mind was miles away from the playbook.

The school rule was you had to attend at least half a day of classes, or you would be ineligible for any game that night. Ali dropped Cody off at school at lunch time.

Cody knew he could not function, nor did he want to be around people. The athletic director met Cody at the doorway and took him into his office. They spoke briefly about the game that night. Cody said he didn't think he could concentrate enough to play the game. He spent the rest of the school day in the office reading about colleges.

His mother told him that Collin would want him to play more than anything. Cody finally agreed to at least try. Even though it was an away game the crowd that evening was aware for Collin's passing and all eyes were on Cody even more than usual. On the first play of the game Cody fumbled the ball. The next series of downs he threw an interception. At halftime they were behind. Alan was standing just outside the locker room door waiting for the team. As Cody started to pass by,

Alan grabbed his arm. Then out of nowhere, Alan started screaming at Cody. He was telling him he was better than what he was playing. "You need to get your head out of your ass! Do you think your dad would be proud of this performance?" Cody swung his arm away, but had a tear in his eye. Alan had never, never even close, talked to him like that in his entire life.

Cody didn't even hear a word the coach said during the halftime talk. He could only hear Alan screaming – "you think your dad is proud of this performance" over and over again.

Cody had something come over him from Alan's "pep talk". During warm-ups for the second half, Cody was all business. He stated yelling at his teammates, pointing and directing. When the second half started, you would have thought the seas were being parted! Cody never threw an incomplete pass the entire second half. He threw 5 touchdown passes and ran for another one. He was playing as if he were possessed. They won the game going away. The opposing coach told the media after the game that he had never seen a performance like that in his 30 plus years of coaching.

CHAPTER 11

The next day was the showing at the local funeral home. When the family arrived three hours early, there were people already lined up outside the door. The family knew this was going to be a very difficult day. There wasn't anything they could have done to prepare for this. As they entered the back door, the funeral director met them. He gave his condolences as he escorted them into the kitchen area.

The entire kitchen area was covered with food. Neighbors, church friends and even complete strangers had dropped off food. Cody just looked at his mother when he seen all the food as if what had happened. Ali just looked at him, "I guess this is their way of grieving for us."

Ali picked at the food, but Cali and Cody didn't even make an attempt. They were escorted into the parlor for the first time. Cody could not take his eyes off the casket in the other end of the room. He didn't want to walk up to it, but his legs kept moving. His sister Cali was squeezing his hand as tight as she could. All three of them were holding back tears as they approached the casket. As Cody looked down, he told his mother that his dad hated neckties, and he shouldn't have one on. She looked into Cody's eyes, then went and got the director asking him to remove the tie.

The doors were opened and as the crowd entered, the first person in line was Alan and his mother, Audrey.

As the day went on, Cody would not leave the head of the casket. He stood there without moving for over 8 hours. Most of the people that came up to Cody spoke highly of Collin, but then turned the conversation over to the previous night's game. All Cody would say, "It was all for him."

After the 8 hours had passed, Cody could see the end of the line. As the last person approached, Cody looked up and saw that it was Alan again. "What are doing back here?" Alan's response , "I just wanted to know if you needed anything." Cody gave him a hug as the front doors were being closed.

The next day was sunny and the turning foliage gave the otherwise dark day color. The funeral services picked up right where the calling stopped. There were so many people that the funeral home could not seat them all. People were outside listening to the service over the speaker.

The drive to the cemetery should have been a short ride. However, Ali wanted the procession to drive past Collin's old high school 15 miles away. Cars were lined up for miles and miles. The thought crossed Ali's mind that most of these people were there for Cody, more so than for remembering Collin.

At the cemetery the service went rather quickly. Everyone departed shortly thereafter. Cody remained seated by the casket finding it difficult to leave. His mother and sister Cali had tried to pull him up, but he wanted to stay a little while longer.

After about 30 minutes, Cody felt a hand on his shoulder. He heard a voice whisper, "Cody, it's time to go." When he turned around, he saw Alan standing there. Cody reached up and touched his hand, then stood up and went to his mother and sister waiting in the car.

CHAPTER 12

The football season had ended two games too soon. They lost in the semi-state final. Even though it wasn't the state championship, it was the furthest the school had ever gone in the tournament. Cody's freshman year had been one for the record books. He was getting the attention of almost every major college in the Midwest. Because of his age, recruiters were not allowed to contact him until his junior year.

As soon as the last game of football had been played, Cody quickly picked up his basketball shoes and hit the hardwood the following Monday. Basketball was his best sport, but baseball was his passion. The basketball team, even though it was made up of mostly the same football players, was not as renowned for their round ball skills. Cody, on the other hand, was in fact one of the better players just as he was on the football field. Cody's god given athletic abilities were kicking into high gear now. His name was already being spread across the Midwest about his record breaking football statistics. His record setting did not stop with football. His first season on the hardwood in high school was matching those on the football field.

Now Cody was being covered by media from all over the state. Some articles were saying that Cody had the potential to be the best athlete to ever come out of the state. Of course Cody's hat size grew after reading these articles. The attention he was receiving would be hard for anyone to handle. It was almost impossible for a 15 year old boy.

The basketball season, and the following baseball season, both had winning records. Cody's freshman year was winding down. At night Cody would pray talking to his dad. He knew in his heart that his dad would be proud of what he had accomplished so far, but the road was still long and unknown.

That summer Cody turned 16. This is a big milestone to any teenager, getting their drivers license. For Cody, as predicted, this also meant a new girl friend.

Ali was able to buy Cody a car from the life insurance money. The money however wasn't enough to live on and raise two kids. She had to take a job at the local grocery store as a cashier, working three nights a week.

Ali didn't want Cody to work during the summer. She wanted him to work out as much as possible. She knew in her heart his only chance for college was an athletic scholarship. His grades were average at best, even with Alan's occasional help.

Cody went to the school every day during the summer. He would lift weights every other day, and run sprints daily. The weights must have done more than build muscle as Cody grew another 3 inches, now equally his dad at 6' 4".

Cody's sophomore year was almost a carbon copy of his freshman season. The football team again lost only one game. Again, they were short of the state championship. All of the players however were starting to enjoy the state wide recognition. Cody's summer regiment was paying off. Even at 16, he was almost like a man upon boys.

The classroom however was another story. The courses were getting more difficult as some were college prep classes. Cody's track record of not being a good student was now catching up with him. He was being left behind and fading fast.

Again he turned to Alan, who like always gladly accepted his "secret mentor" role. This also gave them the chance to play music again in the concealed confines of Cody's basement.

CHAPTER 13

Cody knew that his junior year would be a very important one. This would be the first year that college recruiters could actually contact him. He was looking forward to this process, but he wasn't so sure just what to expect. The athletic director brought in another student athlete he knew that had gone through the recruiting process. He met with Cody and Ali giving them a lot of advice on what to watch for. He was also able to explain a lot of the "do's and don'ts" to them.

As soon as the fall classes began, the letters started arriving at both home and at school. Ali was simply amazed on the quantity. Letters were coming from colleges and universities from all 50 states. He was receiving interest in all three sports.

What surprised Ali more than anything was the fact that none of them seemed concerned about his grade point average.

The coaches were a little concerned on how Cody would handle all the national attention. Cody continued his strong work ethic and seemed to keep everything balanced. His success on the sport scene never diminished. Every game more records fell and his name continued to rise. Again there were no state championships, but winning records in all three sports. Cody made a vow that during his senior year the school would indeed hang a state championship banner from the rafters.

His little sister, Cali, was now in junior high school. They had a show choir called Young Originals. She was excited about trying out as she loved to sing and dance. Cody had made fun of that group when Alan was in it back in their junior high days. Of course when Cali made the choir, Cody told her it was because she was his little sister. Cali was one of the few that were getting real tired of hearing about Cody Tucker!

The following day Alan came over and congratulated Cali on making the show choir. Alan had made the high school show choir, Panache. He was now playing his violin and even singing solo's on stage. Luckily for him, the choir had to wear outfits. If only they had modern glasses!!!!

CHAPTER 14

Cody worked harder than he ever had before during the summer. He had gone through several girlfriends the last three years, but now was only focusing on athletics. He knew this was his last season, and wanted it to be the best. His coaches had always been impressed with his work ethic. But now, he was like a demon possessed.

There were a couple of freshman coming up that Cody was excited about. He had seen them play in junior high while watching Cali cheer. Both played wide receiver, and that was the immediate need for Cody.

For Cali, now in high school, she was the proud sister of Cody. She found herself getting a lot of attention just because she shared the same last name. Her biggest hurdle though was all the boys seemed to be afraid of her, or was it her brother?

Football practice was in full swing. Cody was very excited about this team's potential. The two freshman receivers had made the varsity and Cody was pulling for them to get playing time. Last year's starters had graduated and Cody needed some good hands to throw to.

The first game of the season was against a smaller school, Waveland. Waveland did have a very big talented player, Bowman that was being recruited by local colleges. Cody had known him for years, but only on the football field.

The first play of the season Cody dropped back to pass. While he was in the pocket and watching the freshman run his route, he was hit hard from his blindside. Bowman had made a clean hit up high just as another hit Cody low. There was a loud popping sound; suddenly everything seemed to be dead still. Cody rolled over in pain grasping his knee. Bowman quickly took off his helmet and looked down at Cody. He knew that Cody was hurt, and hurt bad. He dropped to his knees beside Cody lowering his head.

The team trainer came running out onto the field. He was only there a few seconds then motioned for the ambulance parked in the end zone, next to where Collin used to sit.

The crowd, players and broadcaster all sit in silence as the ambulance drove off the field. Cody was lying in the back on the stretcher with a busted knee and a broken heart.

Ali and Cali followed the ambulance to the hospital. They were in the waiting room when Alan and his mother Audrey walked in. They all sit together stunned without speaking.

Several minutes later the emergency doctor came out. He took Ali aside alone.

He told her that he was sending Cody to United Hospital Sports Clinic. He said he thought that his injuries were career threatening, but wanted to get him the best possible treatment.

When Ali told the others of the news, Audrey offered to drive them to the hospital. The hour drive was long and very quiet.

The ambulance with Cody had arrived several minutes earlier. Before they parked the car and made their way into the hospital, the on call specialist had already completed his preliminary check of Cody's knee. Cody was being moved to the x-ray room as Ali approached the desk. The specialist was paged and quickly walked up to the desk. He told Ali that he wanted to get x-rays of the damage. He said he wanted to be sure before telling her anything. Ali was begging for an answer. The doctors' only response was he had a lot of damage.

It was going on two hours before the doctor came back to the waiting room. He asked to speak with Ali in private, but she insisted on staying put, and wanted answers. The doctor made eye contact with everyone in the group which had now grown with the addition of the school principle and athletic director. The doctor said Cody had suffered a torn meniscus, a ripped Achilles tendon and a dislocated patella. Ali, not understanding anything that was just said, looked confused at the doctor and asked, "will he be able to play sports again?" The doctor looked at the others, then back at Ali, "he will recover and have full use of his knee, but he will not be able to compete in competitive sports." The gasp in the waiting room even took the doctor off guard. Within seconds of hearing the news, Ali and Cali were hugging each other and crying as hard as ever before. Alan helped them to the seats along the back wall.

It wasn't long before the news media started showing up at the hospital. Ali was not in any mood for the barrage of questions being fired at her. Alan stood up and walked them outside as if he were going to give them the scoop. Once outside he motioned for the hospital security and had them removed from the premises.

Chapter 15

Cody's surgery was a success. His recovery would be very long and hard, even for an athlete. He had missed attending classes for over 6 weeks. Again, Alan was there for him. Not only would he bring all his homework to him, but he would actually do most of the work as well.

The football team had a losing season for the first time in 4 years. Cody was putting all the blame upon himself and was finding it hard to cope with. He knew that basketball practice had started and he was worried about them as well. Alan would try to change the subject whenever the topic turned to sports.

Cody was back at school, but confined to a wheelchair to get around the hallways. He had several students wanting to help him, but he thought it was mostly so they could get out of class early.

The basketball team was struggling without Cody. Again, Cody was putting the blame on himself. The coach let him talk to the team for motivation the first few games. Those opportunities soon stopped when the coach felt like it was becoming more of a distraction.

Not only did the coach ask him not to speak to the team any longer, Cody also noticed all the college offers had stopped just as fast. A few of the colleges he had been considering even sent withdrawal offers because of his injury. Just about every offer he had received, was now a walk-on opportunity, no scholarship.

It was just a couple of days later when the morning announcement at school was about a senior, receiving a full ride scholarship to an Ivy League School. The principle came on the speaker and announced that Alan Montgomery had been selected for a full ride academic scholarship. Cody could hear the cheers from the other classrooms. Cody was happy for Alan, but would never show it. Cody thought to himself that he had been "one upped" by Alan once again. Cody sat there thinking about all his scholarship offers he had, which were hundreds, and now Alan was being recognized. The next time Cody crossed Alan's path, he just threw up his hand and said "congrats."

The time in the wheelchair was driving Cody insane. His thoughts reflected back to when his dad was confined in a wheelchair and Cody never really thought much about it. Now he could understand some of those frustrations.

One afternoon as classes were letting out, Alan saw Cody in the cafeteria. He ran up to Cody all excited. Cody actually laughed as Alan ran up on him. "What is your problem dude?" Alan looked at him, "I have some news, good news, no great news! The show choir wants us, me and you, to perform at our last performance. Cali told them about the song you wrote, and the fact that we have played it together several times." Cody just wheeled himself away shaking his head.

CHAPTER 16

When Cody got home that evening he went straight after Cali. He was screaming and yelling at her for telling the Panache director about his song. He was also upset that she had told everyone at school about him playing the guitar.

When Ali got home from the grocery store, Cali told her what had happened. Ali thought it was a good thing for Cali to do. She went to Cody and just said she wanted to give her "two cents worth." She told Cody that he was a lot more than an athlete. She said he had talent and that he should use it. Ali told him that she had heard them playing and singing his song several times. She looked at Cody and asked, "why not have some fun your senior year? And besides that, you are really good. How much fun do you think Alan would have playing with you up on that stage?" Just think about it.

Cali was begging Cody at every opportunity. She was in the choir as well and really wanted that memory. She was doing her best "little sister gig" when Cody finally gave in. "One song Cali, tell them one song!"

Even though Cody thought about backing out on several occasions, he stayed true to his promise and was ready to play.

The news blew through the school like a tornado. Cody just kind of pretended it wasn't a big deal at all; he was doing it for his little sis.

The show choir had been doing pretty well in competitions this season. They were drawing in bigger crowds than years before, but still no sell outs. That was about to change. When the word got out that Cody was playing, all seats were gone within two days. They all wanted to support Cody, no matter if he could sing or not, because of what he had gone through.

The night of the performance was upon them. Cody found he was more nervous for this than any sporting event he had ever competed in. The show was over and they were going to close the night out. First Alan walked out carrying his violin. Then the spotlight turned to the corner of the stage as Cody was being pushed out in his wheelchair by his sister Cali. The crowd cheered as they came onto the stage.

Cody took the microphone and looked at the audience. "Glad you guys clapped now because you won't be when we are finished!" The laughter could be heard across the street.

Alan took the microphone. He looked at the crowd, then to Cody. I wanted to say thank you for doing this my friend. Cody raised his hand and they shook publicly for the first time.

Alan turned to the crowd and told them they were going to play a song that Cody had written after his father had passed. The song is titled, "My Friend."

Alan placed the microphone onto the stand, and adjusted it to Cody's guitar.

Alan then stepped back and began playing his violin soft and low. Cody soon joined in the chorus and the crowd was as quiet as the night when Cody got hurt. Cody's deep voice began to sing and not a person moved. Cody was singing from his heart and stunning the crowd.

As Cody strummed the last cord and looked up into the spotlight, tears could be seen running down his cheeks. The applause began as a ripple because the audience were also busy getting napkins, hanker-chiefs, anything they could find to wipe their own tears. Then the applause continued to grow into a roar. The crowd stood on their feet. Cody motioned for Cali. When she got beside him, he handed her his guitar and slowly stood on his own feet. He raised his hand and covered his heart. Then he slowly bowed to the crowd. The crowd continued with their applause as he sat back down and Cali wheeled him off the stage.

The next day at school all of the talk was about "the performance" from the night before. Cody was still getting out of class early to avoid the crowd in his wheelchair. The first period was about to end and Cody was being escorted towards his next class when the Panache director approached him in the hallway. She wanted to tell him how proud she was of his performance. Cody just looked up at her and said it was like an out of body experience. She told him that she thought he had a lot of potential in music, both singing and writing. She asked if he had ever thought about going that direction. Cody just kind of laughed, saying "not really, mom and Cali are the singers of the family."

CHAPTER 17

The following Monday evening Cody received a telephone call. Ali had answered and didn't recognize the voice on the other end. She handed Cody the phone and for a brief moment just stood there making sure everything was fine. Cody gave her a little wave and she walked away. The man on the other end was from the local radio station. Someone had taken a video of the performance to the station and wanted them to review it. At first Cody was upset that someone would do that. The station wanted permission to play the song even though the quality wasn't the best from a home video. Cody quickly put that to rest saying NO.

The next morning at school Cody learned that the school had videotaped the entire Panache show (something they always done), and the school had in fact sent the tape to the station. They apologized for not asking Cody's permission. They said they just wanted his song to be heard.

The following weekend Alan came over to his house. Cody had been gone just about every evening during the week for rehab. He was close to getting out of the chair and onto crutches.

Alan found Cody in front of the TV watching the first baseball game of the season. After some small talk, Alan handed him a package. Cody looked up at him, "what the heck is this?" Alan just said, "why don't you open it and find out?" Cody ripped the envelope open and pulled out a packet of papers. The cover sheet had pictures of young performers on stage. This was an entry form for an upcoming talent show at the state capitol. This was a national audition for a new talent show called "New Country." Cody just laughed, handed back the packet and said "good luck with that." Alan looked at him, "it's not for me. I brought it here for you. You have the talent. You have the potential, why not try it? Just what do you have to lose?" Alan sat the envelope down and went home. Cody went back to the game on TV, but his eyes would creep over to the packet during commercials.

Cody was at rehab with his mother. He stood and stepped from his wheelchair for the final time. The specialist handed Cody his crutches. Cody looked at her, "would you do me a favor and kick the chair?" He let out a laugh as she did.

Cody made his way on his new crutches to the car. Ali started the car and asked if he wanted to go anywhere special, now that the chair wasn't attached to him. Cody looked at her, "home sounds good to me."

While driving back home Cody looked at his mom. "I want to ask you a serious question. Now I mean I want you to be completely honest with me- 100 percent!"

Ali, looking at him somewhat confused, shook her head yes. "Yes, sure, you know I will. I always have been." "Do you think I am good singer? BE HONEST MOM!"

Ali, trying to keep her eyes on the road, again shook her head yes. "You know I think you are good. I have always told you that. Why are you asking?" "Alan wants me to audition for a talent show. I have been thinking about it a lot. I have lost all my scholarships to college, my grades aren't the best, and besides that, you can't afford to send me anyway. So, I am thinking about it. Do you think I should?"

Ali did not hesitate, "yes you should Cody. You have talent." Not a word was said the rest of the way home.

Cody walked slowly on his new means of transportation to his room. He flopped down on his bed and looked at the audition form. Then he leaned over and reached into his dresser drawer and pulled out a shoe box. He started pulling out stacks of torn and folded papers. All of these were songs he had written over the years. After reading through them, he couldn't help but think about his dad. He remembered telling his father on his death bed that he would make something of himself. Of course they both thought that was going to be sports. Now with sports gone from his life, Cody looked to the ceiling and spoke out loud, "this is my chance."

He filled out the form and the next morning it found its way into the mailbox.

Chapter 18

Graduation was this coming Friday. The senior class had finally made their way through. Everyone was excited about starting their next venture of life. Cody, now walking with only one crutch, was glad to see the end in sight. His high school athletic career was mostly a blur to him. He was "living a dream" until that frightful night on the football field. He often thought about the injury. He wasn't honestly sure who would have suffered more if his dad had been alive to see it.

As his name was announced and he slowly climbed the side stairs with his crutch, the audience cheered and clapped as if he were their own child. The principle made his way to the side to assist him at the top stair. After receiving his diploma, Cody gave a quick glance to the crowd and had flashbacks of his basketball days. A smile crossed his face, as he raised his hand covering his heart and giving a final wave.

Alan was getting ready for his move to college. This was going to be a big move for him. He had never been away from his mother, Audrey. His father, Clyde on the other hand, he hardly even knew.

Alan made his way over to Cody's house just a few days prior to leaving. He had been asking Cody about the audition for several weeks. Cody still had not heard anything back and was mentally giving up before it even started. Alan was obviously having a hard time saying goodbye to Cody. He never could relate to him very well, always being kept at arm's length. He finally just looked at Cody and said good luck. Cody didn't even stand from the couch, his only response back was, "yeah you too." Alan left hoping for a lot more than that from him.

Two days after Alan had left Cody received a letter in the mail. It was from the talent show. Cody couldn't open it. He took it to his mother and asked her to open it in the other room. She walked out with the package. Within minutes she walked back in trying her best to hold back her emotions. She handed Cody the package. She sat down beside him, put her arm around him, and whispered into his ear. "Cody, looks like you MADE IT!" She immediately started jumping up and down. Cody's smile told it all. He really did want this, but he was afraid to show it.

That evening they were going over song choices. Ali finally took charge. "Cody, there really is only one choice. Sing the song from your heart. You got to sing "My Friend" in your audition." Cody agreed.

Cody had only had 10 days to get prepared for his tryout. He wasn't worried about the time frame he felt he was "good to go."

CHAPTER 19

Ali told Audrey about the upcoming audition so she could let Alan know. Even though Cody wanted to keep it quiet around town, little sister Cali had other plans. She was telling everyone, even the radio station. Soon the town was buzzing about Cody. Everyone knew that he was good, and all of them were hoping for the best. Soon posters were in store front windows and ribbons tied around trees.

Cody just shook his head. He was used to the "limelight" but he thought this was a bit much.

The day before the audition, Cody went to his dad's grave site. He had made many trips before, but this time it felt different. He was worried about what his dad would think. He always made fun of singers and dancers, and now, his only son was trying that route. Cody was in search of some type of answer, but it never came that afternoon. Just before walking away from the grave, Cody raised his hand and covered his heart, and waved towards the sky. Be with me my friend; please be with me he whispered as he walked away.

When Cody arrived for the audition he found thousands of people there in line. At first he thought he had to wait in line like the rest of them. When he approached the sign in table, he was given a number to attach to his chest, and was escorted into the building. He asked the assistant what the line was about. He was informed those were the people that are just hoping for a tryout, they had not been invited.

Once inside he found long lines of tables and people running around everywhere with walkie-talkies. Soon he was taken to another room with only 5 other people.

Another person came in and told them what to expect. They were advised that when called, they needed to walk through the adjacent door, and that's where the judges were. They were supposed to introduce themselves, tell them the name of the song they were going to sing, then sing until they were stopped. This person told them to expect to sing three or four lines. Then the briefing was over and just as fast, one of the five was called in. Cody was used to performing, but not like this. He was in fact getting nervous.

The guy called in came out rather quickly. His look of dejection told his story. He walked by Cody whispering, "they didn't even give me a chance!"

The next person called in, a cute long haired blonde, was in the audition a little longer, but she too came out long faced and teary eyed.

Then they called for Cody. He took a deep breath then walked through the door. As he walked to center stage, he looked out and saw three judges. He didn't recognize any of them. He was asked if he thought he could make it through and win the contest. Cody hesitated, and then answered "well my mom thinks so!" All of them laughed. They asked what song he was going to sing, he answered a song titled "My Friend." One of the judges asked "who is that by?" Cody answered, "me." The judge quickly responded "no, I mean who wrote that song?" Cody, grinning now, again answered, "me."

He strummed his guitar and started singing. Again it was easy to sing from the heart when it was about his best friend, his father Collin. Cody didn't even realize that when he had finished, he had played the entire song. Two of the judges sat there with open mouths. The third started clapping, soon joined by the other two.

Without question, Cody was passed through to the next round. He walked out stunned. Ali and Cali were waiting for him in the waiting room. Cody had a blank look on his face as he walked out and Ali wasn't sure if that was a good sign or a bad one. He then handed her the pass for the next round. Cali jumped on him, making Cody wince as his leg was in a bind.

When he got home, he had a message from Alan. Alan wanted to know about the audition and wanted Cody to call him back as soon as he got home. Alan left his number, but Cody never called it.

CHAPTER 20

Thanks to Cali, the results of the audition travelled quickly throughout the town.

Cody couldn't understand the phenomena of the whole thing. He told his mother, "I only passed the first round, what's the big deal?"

The following week was the second round, held in the same location, same judges. Only this time they had to sing a song picked out for them by the judges.

They would only have two hours to practice prior to the audition.

Cody arrived, still nervous, but this time because he didn't have a clue what song he would have to perform. He went to the desk and got signed in. When he was given his number, he looked down and saw number 14. That was his number all through high school in every sport. His lips curled in a slight grin. He walked into a large holding room joining the overflow crowd of contestants. All of them were anxiously awaiting their song titles. He closed his eyes, and again whispered, be with me my friend, please be with me. One of the assistants walked up and handed him an envelope. It was his song title, and he had two hours to the minute, then he would have to perform it. He opened the envelope and pulled out the paper.

As he turned it over, he saw the title "Love Me" by Collin Raye. Cody had tears in his eyes as he looked to the ceiling. He knew he would be "good to go."

Cody was called in and went to center stage. One of the judges said he had picked this song for him since his last song was a ballad, this seemed to be his forte'.

Cody tired to sing the song to his dad, and it came through just that way once more. They let him sing the entire song. When he had finished, the head judge just looked at him. "Cody, without question, you are one of the best I have ever heard. Son, you are well on your way. Congratulations."

As Cody walked out of the room this time, there was no doubt in anyone's eyes the results he had just been given. Cali was on her cell phone before she even hugged Cody!

Alan had heard the news from the first audition from his mother. He again called Cody from school leaving his phone number. He wanted to know as soon as possible on the results of round two. Alan's results were the same, Cody never called.

CHAPTER 21

Now the town was in total chaos. The town was pretty much on fire and Cali was the fuel. Cody could not even leave the house without people taking pictures, following him wherever he went, and nonstop phone calls.

Cody was now one of the three finalists. Now the judging was up to the fans. Cody knew his chances of winning the contest were very low since he lived in a smaller market then the other two finalists. One was a very cute female from Los Angeles, and the other was a male from Houston.

At the final competition, they could sing any song they wanted to. Cody wrestled with his choices. He knew he should sing a popular song, but at times that seemed to hurt people's chances as they are compared to the original performer. So he decided to sing another song he had written back in high school. This was a big opportunity for him, and he wasn't sure about his choice. After going back and forth what seemed to be a thousand times, he chose one of his songs titled "Listen To Me."

It was show time and it was being broadcasted on national TV for the first time. All three of the contestants became friends behind the scenes. None of them thought they would win it! They had a drawing back stage for the order of performance. Cody drew number two.

The first performer, the female, sang a Martina McBride song and absolutely nailed it. Cody knew right then she would be the winner. Before he took stage, he covered his heart and looked up whispering, be with me my friend, please be with me. As he took center stage, camera front, he gave his name once again and the song title he was about to perform. He said it was a song that nobody would know, as he wrote it and it had never been sung publicly before tonight.

The song, once again coming from within, came out as if it had been recorded and already on the charts. Cody felt good about the performance, but now it was all up to the voters across America. The third contestant sang well, but Cody still felt that the female had won the contest.

The next night was the results show. The first person named would be the third place finisher. The guy from Houston was announced. Cody took a deep breath, hoping for the best. They next announced the winner. Cody's gut feeling was right. The female had won the contest, Cody finishing second.

The crowd made it known that they didn't necessarily agree with the results. The judges were given an opportunity to talk to all three. All three contestants were given encouragement. The head judge congratulated all three, and then turned his attention to Cody. "Cody, you may not have won this contest, but you have won a lot of hearts across this country. I predict you will do well, and I mean very well in this business."

When Cody arrived back home, the town looked as though he had won the contest.

He looked at his mother, "what the heck? I didn't even win!"

When he got to the house, for the third time he had a message from Alan. He was begging Cody to call him back. Again, Cody ignored the request.

They had a press conference set up for him the next day at the school. Cody just scratched his head in disbelief.

At the press conference he thanked everyone for their support and calling in votes for him. He had hoped this experience had been good for everyone. He was thankful that his small hometown had received some national attention.

During the press conference a tall, well dressed man approached the stage. He took the microphone off the stand and stood beside Cody. He said he was with Renner Records out of Nashville Tennessee. He said he was there to offer Cody a contract to write and sing for their label. The entire crowd went berserk! Cody was stunned and had to take a step back. His emotions ran straight to his face and he could hardly speak a word. Taking the microphone, all he could say was "thank you."

Cody's signing made national news. Just as the one judge had predicted, Cody was on his way. Alan saw the evening news and was celebrating at school for Cody.

He was telling all his classmates that he was best friends with Cody. They didn't believe him, so he called the house once again. Cody wasn't there, and once again, never returned his call.

Chapter 22

Cody was packing his car for the trip south to Nashville when the mailman walked up beside his car. He said he had a letter for him. He wanted to make sure he got it before climbing into his car and heading out to "become a major star." Cody snatched the letter from his friend and said, "yeah you want an autograph?"

Both of them laughed. Cody looked at the letter and saw it was from Alan. He threw the letter into the backseat without opening it.

He said his goodbyes to mom and Cali, then headed out for his unknown future.

On the seven hour drive to Nashville, Cody kept turning the radio to country stations. He would sing along, and then his mind was race ahead thinking that maybe soon his songs would be playing on the radio.

He got to his hotel and called Ali, letting her know he had in fact made it ok. The next day he was to meet with the representative from Renner Records in the hotel lobby.

Cody, who was yet to turn 18, was out on his own and ready for the adventure. He had to have several papers signed by his mother for him to even sign the contract with Renner.

The next morning Cody arose early and headed to the lobby not knowing what to expect. He was met by a man that appeared to be in his mid fifties. He introduced himself, and then off they went to the main office downtown Nashville. Cody's eyes were bouncing all over the place as they drove downtown.

At the office, they had more paperwork to fill out and contractual agreements. After the paper shuffle had settled, they left the office and drove to a studio. When they entered, Cody saw three guys with guitars sitting around a large round table. All of them were song writers. They went around the table introducing themselves one at a time. They grabbed a fourth chair and placed it up to the table. "Have a seat," one of them said as the driver left the room. They all talked about themselves and their backgrounds. They wanted to know about Cody and what Cody was all about. The rest of the afternoon was mostly a meet and greet session.

The next day at the studio, the group wanted to hear Cody sing. He grabbed his guitar and played "My Friend" for them. When he had finished, they all clapped. One of them asked, "did you really write that?" Cody just nodded his head yes.

One of them got up and made a phone call right away. Within minutes a guy walked through the door. He requested that Cody play it again. Cody gladly picked up his guitar and sang it again. When he had finished, they guy asked for him to sing it one more time, only this time he wanted the other three to play behind him. After singing it three more times, Cody was asked if he would record that song. He just laughed and said, "well yeah, that's what I'm here for."

The recording session was set up for the very next day. That would be Cody's third day in Nashville. The session ended up taking most of the day as they continued to change the arrangement. Finally, they had it. The playback blew Cody's mind. All the background music and vocals had polished his song to perfection. Cody couldn't believe that it was his song.

The record was cut as a single. The process for it to hit the market would take several weeks. In the meantime, Cody was fitting in nicely with the other songwriters. All of them were bouncing ideas during each brainstorming session.

Cody had all his songs he had written growing up, but he didn't want to play all his cards too quickly. He didn't have any idea what the future would bring him.

He called his mom every night. He made her promise not to tell Cali about cutting "My Friend" until it came out. She said she would, and she did keep her word.

During the next few weeks, Cody would go to Printers Alley and perform for free practicing some of the new songs, and throwing in some of his old ones. He was having a lot of fun doing this, but he was obligated to Renner Records, so he couldn't get paid. During this time he knew his music was being accepted.

Finally release day arrived. Renner Records didn't drop a lot of money on this project since Cody was still so new. The public knew him from the show, but they had to walk slowly with him. The song was soon getting air time. When Cody first heard it on the radio he actually cried.

CHAPTER 23

"My Friend" was growing legs as they say in the business.
Every country radio station in the nation was now playing
it on their daily rotation. Cody was getting comfortable
now with the group and opened up even more. He started
bringing in other previous songs that he had written as
"My Friend" continued climbing the chart.

The record label decided to cut another one of Cody's
songs, "Listen To Me."

He had played that during the competition and
everyone seemed to love it.

Just as "My Friend" broke into the top 40, "Listen To Me" was released, two weeks after Cody's 18th birthday.

"My Friend" peaked at 26, just outside the top 25. It had received a great deal of air time, and it firmly placed Cody's feet within the country music industry.

"Listen To Me" also had a great run for Cody. This single peaked at 20, making Americas Top 20 Country chart. This also put his name in the running for Newcomer of the Year in country music. However, this was one reward that would escape him.

Renner Records wanted Cody to do some local performances to work on his stage presence. They booked him around Nashville, but this time he was getting paid. He continued working the smaller clubs the rest of the summer.

The group was just amazed on how he could find the words at such a young age. All of them were well into their late 30's and early 40's. They would meet every Monday and Wednesday to write. Cody was performing 6 nights a week now.

Cody found he was just as comfortable on stage, as he was playing sports. Everyone that saw him said the same thing, that he was simply a natural.

CHAPTER 24

Cody was getting consumed with work. His calls to home were getting less and less. Ali was lucky to hear from Cody once a week now. He always made her feel bad when she tried calling him. He always told her that she was calling at a real bad time, so she just stopped calling, even though it hurt.

His name was growing like the ditch weed of the south. His face was starting to appear on billboards and local commercials.

The following spring Renner Records had a corporate meeting. All of the entertainers on their label had to be present. Cody was excited as he was going to meet a lot of them for the first time. During the meeting, Renner announced the scheduled tours for the following summer. Cody was shocked when he learned he had been scheduled for the opening act for a major headliner. In his mind, he had made it. He called his mother right away. The tour was going to be 28 shows in 24 different states. He told her, "I am living the dream."

The deadline for the show was fast approaching. Cody was busy writing new material and working hard with the writers. One of Cody's biggest disappointments however was they had written a great new song together, but it went to the headliner instead. Even though Cody's name was listed as a writer, he was still somewhat disenchanted. The disenchantment soon disappeared as the song became a number one hit and he found out as a writer he got royalties. He actually ended up making more money as a writer for the number one song than he had as a writer/ singer for a number twenty.

The day had arrived when the tour buses pulled out of Nashville. The record label had rented two travel buses for the tour. One bus was for the headliner and band, and the other one was for Cody and his band. A semi followed the buses with all the sound equipment and stage.

Their first stop wasn't far, just south down the interstate to Atlanta. This would be Cody's first performance as a professional in such a large arena. He called his mom from back stage just prior to going on. After hanging up, he raised his hand and covered his heart as he looked up. Again he whispered, "be with me my friend, please be with me."

Cody bounced onto the stage to an excited crowd. He began playing his songs and the crowd was responding to every word. Cody performed eight songs, introduced the headliner, and then sat back stage to watch the show. Cody was indeed, on his way.

CHAPTER 25

The tour was going along without a hitch. Every show was better than the previous one. Everything was falling into place for Cody. Of course back home Cali, now being a sophomore, was now living her own dream being the little sister of Cody Tucker!

The rest of the tour was a resounding success. On the last night of the show, Renner Records Executives were back stage. Cody was told this was normal that they always came to the last show of the tour. When the show was over, they asked Cody to meet with them in his bus.

Cody didn't have any idea what was up. When he entered the bus, there were three executives present. He sat down nervously at the table with them on the other side.

They congratulated him on the tour, and his success he was having on the charts.

They asked him how he felt about the tour, and his response was it was fantastic.

They said they agreed and had an offer for him. Cody's eyes widened and he sat upright at the table. "And what's that?" he asked. They pulled out a new contract from their briefcase. Cody, here is a new contract with Renner Records, and we want you to be one of our headliners next year. Cody just sat there starring at them. "This is a joke right? Where is the hidden camera?" They shook their heads, no joke Cody, this is serious. Look at the contract and you will see just how serious we are. Cody took the contract and his eyes planted directly on the dollar figure. The contract was for one million dollars, plus royalties. Cody sat there with his eyes glued to the paperwork. He didn't know what to say. Cody, this is a nice contract for you and your family. But understand one thing, this isn't nearly as big as some of the other performers we have. You have potential to grow son. Cody's eyes were glazed over with tears. He reached out his hand, "give me a pen!"

Cody signed the contract, and called his mother before the ink had even dried. His first thing out of his mouth after telling her the dollar amount was Cali would now have her college education taken care of.

The following week Cody was back at the studio writing with the others. They had all heard the news and were hoping this wouldn't affect Cody's writing abilities. He walked in and sat down as if nothing had happened. In fact, he didn't even mention it the entire day. It was just business as usual.

The next day Cody came in with a song that he had written the night before. He had written the entire song lyrics, now they just needed the track. Before the day was over, they had another great song on their hands. However this time, the song was staying with Cody.

Cody told them that the song just came to him. He said it was one that just had to be written. He told them he picked up the pen and didn't set it down until the song was finished. All of them just shook their heads in amazement.

The following day, "Forgiven" was recorded. The label company wanted to "sit" on this one until it was closer for his tour to begin. They all knew this was going to be a big hit. Even though it upset Cody about "sitting" on it, he agreed and knew they were right.

CHAPTER 26

As winter came in Cody was able to get back home for the first time in months.

He had tried staying in contact with his mother as much as he could, but he knew it wasn't nearly enough. Even though she didn't like it, she was learning to adjust to his busy lifestyle.

He told his mom about the song, "Forgiven." He said he knew it would be a big hit. He was actually predicting for a number one out of it.

Cali was bugging him about signing at the school for a special needs child. She just didn't understand that he couldn't do that because he was under contract.

He said he could go and sign autographs, and take pictures, but he could not sing.

So he ended up spending the entire day with Cali at the school having his picture taken over and over again. He was getting writers cramps before the day was through, but he knew it was for a good cause.

Cody was able to spend the next three weeks with his mother and sister for the holidays. He knew those times would be hard to come by in the near future.

The second Monday in January he was back in Nashville with the group at the roundtable. The schedule for the upcoming tour was almost complete. The song "Forgiven" was going to be released in two weeks. Cody was ready to see just where that song would finally land.

The day had come for the upcoming tour schedule to be released. The tour was a six month schedule, covering thirty cities. This was a very difficult schedule for any entertainer, let alone a brand new headliner. But the true irony of this tour was Cody's opening act. It was the winner of the contest he was in, the girl from LA.

She had just signed a contract with Renner and they thought she would help promote Cody's tour. Cody was glad to see it as they had already become friends from the contest days.

Chapter 27

The first stop of the tour was in Boston. Cody had prepared well for this tour and was more than ready to be a headliner.

The opening night went well. The only hiccup was the opening act had some sound equipment issues. Those were soon fixed and the show went on without any other problems.

The next night was a performance in New York City. Cody had never played there and wasn't sure about his name and recognition. The line outside Madison

Square Garden soon put all that to rest. The new release, "Forgiven" had screamed into the top 10 the first week of the tour. The song was still climbing just as Cody predicted. He saw his picture on Time Square reinforcing his thoughts, "I have made it. I am living a dream."

When the show was over, one of the crew members approached Cody and said there was a guy that wanted to see him, and that it was important. Cody asked who it was. Not sure was the response, but he seemed genuine.

Cody walked out of the back and walked right into Alan. "ALAN?" Alan stuck out his hand towards Cody. Cody shook his hand, "man it's been awhile!" Alan said that it had been. He said he had called him several times but never got a call back.

Cody's only response was, "I don't call mom like I should either."

Alan looked at him and Cody could tell something wasn't right. "What's up Alan?"

Alan had a hard time looking at him when he spoke. "Well, to be honest this isn't going to be easy to say. Cody, I have been diagnosed with leukemia. It's progressed and they tell me that I am not good. I wanted you to know. I have tried calling you but you haven't returned any of my calls. I knew this was the only way to tell you, in person. My mom and dad are the only other people that know about this."

Cody invited Alan back to his bus. They talked about old times and how funny it was that Cody was playing music for a living. Alan looked at him, "long way from the basement huh? You wanted to play professional sports, and now you are playing music. I wanted to be a lawyer, now I am dying! Some hand I was dealt huh?"

The tour bus had to pull out to make the next nights show in Chicago. Cody told them to go on and that he would fly over. He got a hotel rooms for them that night. They went to a restaurant to get something to eat and talk. Alan thought it was funny that Cody was actually noticed by fans and had to sign a few autographs. Alan looked at him smiling, "if only they knew." Cody just looked at him, "shut up."

They remained at the restaurant well after midnight just talking about old times.

Alan kept telling him about all the times he had reached out to Cody. Cody, listening for several minutes finally spoke up. You were always there for me all along weren't you? Every time something happened to me, every time, you were there.

"Why didn't I see that Alan? Why?" Alan told him that he was there for him all along and he would be as long as he was alive. The restaurant was closing down and they had to leave. They got to their hotel rooms knowing Cody had to catch an early flight. Alan stuck out his hand and Cody grabbed it and pulled him into a hug. Alan whispered into his ear, I was there all along for you. I always will be. They parted their hug. Alan quickly covered his heart with his hand then waved it at Cody. "Make us proud Cody!" He walked into his room and Cody watched the door shut. That was the last time Cody ever saw Alan. Alan died later that summer during his tour. Cody didn't even know about his death until after the funeral had already taken place. When he heard the news he had to sit down. He felt a blow to his stomach that reminded him of his football days. Flashes of childhood memories danced in his head. He just couldn't shake the thought that Alan had passed. He had lost a true friend that he hadn't even really known. Cody thought to himself, "I have learned more about Alan in his death than I had during his life!"

The next day should have been one for celebration. His song "Forgiven" had hit number one. But his mind and thoughts were all about Alan. During the show that night he mentioned Alan to the crowd.

He wanted to dedicate the show to Alan's name. He said "if it weren't for Alan Montgomery, I would not be standing before you here today." He asked them all to stand, cover their hearts, and wave to the sky.

That very night on the tour bus as it rolled towards the next city, Cody was reflecting on his last night with Alan. He kept hearing the words, all along. He quickly grabbed a pen and began writing. And just like the last time he had a hit, he didn't put the pen down until he was finished. Cody new this was his best song yet. He recorded the song within two weeks while on the road. He knew he had to get it out as soon as he could. When the song hit the stores, the writer was none other than Alan Montgomery. The song went to number one quicker than any country song in history. It went on to become the biggest selling country single of all time. The song was simply titled – ALL ALONG.

All of the proceeds from this song went to Alan's family. Cody started a scholarship at their high school.

He wanted a fund to help those who helped others. He named the fund, Alan's Foundation. After all, he was there all along.

About the Author

Rick W. French's first published work was in poetry. This is his first fictional short story. Rick is retired from the law enforcement field and is presently working in retail management. Rick and his wife Charli live in Avon, Indiana.

rwfrench14@yahoo.comn